BIG MONTY AND THE CYBORG SUBSTITUTE

Printed in the United States of America
First Printing, 2019

ISBN: 978-1-7337435-7-0

BY
MATT MAXX

Dedication
This book was created in part by
contributions from
SOMBA: Starkville Oktibbeha Minority
Business Alliance

Table of Contents

CHAPTER 1

Experiment Fridays and One Shocking Sub

Fridays popped like the 4th of July in the fifth-grade. On Fridays, Mrs. Curie exploded balloons and blew up volcanoes, all in the name of science! Just about any kind of science is lit. But, if you ask me, astronomy is the coolest. Astronomy is a science that studies space.

Hold up. Let me introduce myself. If you didn't already know, my real name is Merlin, but everyone calls me Big Monty. I am a science fan, one hundred percent. Listen, I know what you're thinking. Who is this nerd? As far as I'm concerned, nerd equals big salary, AKA paycheck. I plan to laugh all the way to the bank when I grow up, but first, I have to get through grade school. As you're about to see, Washington Carver Elementary School is no easy place to survive!

On this particular Friday, I woke up with a banging headache, and my face felt hot. I went to school anyway. It was going to take a lot more than a little fever to keep me away from Mrs. Curie's experiments. Who doesn't like exploding things? One time, Mrs. Curie let us make pop rockets that shot all over the playground!

I kinda had to keep my enthusiasm on the down low. If you got too hyped up about school, kids like A'Lo would start joking on you. A'lo is short for Antivius LaRoyce Jenkins, and he is one bad little joker. I don't see how A'Lo and his buddies stayed unimpressed with Mrs. Curie's experiments. Maybe they just hid their excitement. It was hard to hide mine. I mean, science? Dude, that's my thing. Meet me at the end of the chapter if science is your thing, too.

My buddy Global loved Fridays as much as I did. Global didn't even try to hide his excitement about experiment day. Dude was sitting in the front row wearing plastic goggles and waiting for class to start when I walked in. "Good morning, Big Merlin, I mean Big Monty," Global greeted me with a smile as goofy as those plastic goggles.

I sat behind him. We've been friends since kindergarten, but he's killing his rep with those mad scientist goggles, and he's killing my rep because he can't even remember his best friend's nickname. Sometimes, I don't know how he can be so smart and so clueless at the same time. I looked over my shoulder. A'lo was drooling all over his desk in the back row, sleeping like a dead man.

"I believe today we will be testing the pH levels of common household items," Global said, pointing to the materials on Mrs. Curie's lab table. "pH levels demonstrate how acid or alkaline something is."

I was going to have to look that one up when I got home. Global was beyond me on this one. "Is there anything explosive about that, Global?" I asked. "You really think you need the goggles?"

"Safety cannot be assumed in science," Global quoted from the eighth-grade textbook that he borrowed from his brother's Summer Scholars program.

Sometimes, Global is even too much for me. I was just glad A'lo was sleeping, so I didn't have to hear lame "yo' mama" jokes about science nerds. I could hear A'lo's short self now, "Yo' mama's glasses are so thick, she can see into another dimension . . . hahahaha!"

All of a sudden, the classroom door opened, and instead of Mrs. Curie's white lab coat and high heels, a tall dude strolled in. He looked like a retired NFL player who had gone soft. A scar ran down the side of his face that reminded me of the scary movie I watched when I wasn't supposed to, but that wasn't the worst. He was clutching a stack of papers and books on his left side with something that looked like a robot hand.

"What the what?" I looked at Global.

"James Bond hand, like in the movies my dad loves," Global said. "The Man with the Silver Arm!"

Yo. Glad you showed up! I told you about some of the cool experiments Mrs. Curie did in class, right? Check out this one you can do at home. Make sure your parents are around because you have to use fire, and there is no way your mama is going to believe it was worth you burning down the kitchen just to learn some physics!

This experiment is called Egg in a Bottle, and it shows the relationship between pressure and temperature. Pressure can mean someone trying to convince you to do something, like when your mama puts pressure on you to clean your room, or she won't take you to the movies. In this experiment, pressure means the continuous physical force exerted on an object by something in contact with it. Let's break that down. Exerted means to make a physical or mental effort, like when you exert your brain by studying for a math test.

It turns out, as you'll see in this experiment, temperature affects how much force is exerted on the egg.

The Great Egg Suck Experiment

Here's what you'll need to see it for yourself:

Adult supervision

Glass container with a mouth smaller than the egg

Hard boiled eggs (peeled)

Matches or lighter

Strips of paper

Here's what you do:

1. Find a glass jar with an opening at least half the diameter of the egg — diameter is how big around it is at its widest part.
2. If you have it, rub vegetable oil around the inside of the jar opening.
3. Use a match or lighter to light the end of a strip of paper on fire, and drop it in the bottle.
4. Put the egg on the mouth of the bottle, and watch what happens!

Here's why it works:

Before you light the paper, the air pressure inside the bottle is the same as the air pressure outside the bottle. Once you heat it up, the air molecules inside the bottle expand or get bigger. That expanding air puts pressure on the egg to move out of the way, so it can escape from the bottle and have more room, which makes the egg vibrate or shake. When the flame went out after it consumed all the oxygen in the bottle, the air inside the bottle cooled down.

Did you know that fire needs oxygen to live just like we do? Cool air takes up less space which creates less pressure inside the bottle. The egg was blocking extra air

from outside the bottle from getting in.
That caused an unbalanced force. The force
of the air pushing on the egg from outside
the bottle was greater than the force of
air pushing up on it from inside the bottle.
And, BOOM! The egg was pushed inside
the bottle!

If you want to know how to get the egg
out of the bottle without making a giant
mess, look up Bill Nye The Science Guy
and Sucking Eggs on YouTube. I know you
laughed at Sucking Eggs! See? Science isn't
all serious.

CHAPTER 2

All Jokes and No Laughs

The substitute teacher slammed his stack of papers down on Mrs. Curie's desk, whirled around, and glared at us from under his fat, hairy caterpillar eyebrows. Janet Ellis fell out of her chair and swallowed her gum. Everyone else sat at full attention like army recruits. That is, everyone but A'lo, who snored.

I expected him to growl at us in some super villain voice, but the substitute cracked a goofy grin that made his scar crinkle up and said, "Gooooooood mooooooooorning, Kindy-garteners!"

Global turned to me, confused, and shrugged his shoulders, "Kindy-garteners?"

"Who knows why you can't trust atoms," the sub bellowed. Even Global was coming up with nothing on this one. "Anyone? Anyone?" The oversized substitute waved his silver hand around like a giant crossing guard while he waited for an answer.

"Because they make up EVERYTHING!" He roared and bent over laughing so hard that he started wheezing.

"I believe there is something not quite right with this man," Global whispered back to me.

"Ya' think?" I shook my head which was beginning to ache even more than it had this morning. "Dude is completely unhinged!"

When no one laughed at his joke, the sub tried another tactic. "Forgive me class, I neglected to introduce myself. I am Colonel Freezo Freezingberg, and I am your substitute for today. You may call me Col. Freezingberg, Sir Freezo, Freezo, or just The Freeze." He paused for an uncomfortably long time and stared into every one of our faces. Here was a guy who had more trouble with his nickname than I did.

"Everybody up!" he commanded, pounding his iron fist against the lab table. We all stood up slowly beside our chairs, except A'lo, who was totally out of it. Jamal Tanner looked like he was pointing his track shoes toward the door, ready to run for it.

Colonel Freezo pulled out his phone and turned up the volume. He whipped out a Raiders cap from his back pocket and cocked it sideways on his head. All of a sudden, a theme show song for preschoolers started blaring out of the phone's speaker.

"Is that . . . the Barney theme song?" I asked in disbelief.

"Let's get our blood flowing to my ringtone!" Freezo shouted as he began to do some crazed line-dance at the front of the room. No one moved.

It took him a while to notice that he was the only one dancing. "Well," he clicked off the music," looks like I have a serious set of scientists on my hands."

He lumbered over to Mrs. Curie's lab materials. Then, he grabbed his water bottle and slurped the whole thing down in one gulp, spilling it all down the front of his shirt. "Let's get on with the magic of CHEMISTRY!" Freezo boomed, waving his arms in the air like he was at a concert.

"You," he pointed to Global. "Pass out the instructions." Global looked nervous as he took crumpled papers from Freezo's metal claw. While Global was passing out the instructions, Sir Freezo pulled out a bunch of vials full of unknown substances from the pockets on his cargo pants.

"We are going to add a few ingredients to spice this experiment up!" Freezo began mixing some of the colorful liquids from his vials into a beaker.

"Dude," I whispered to Global once he sat back down, "What is this weirdo doing?"

"This is not in the protocol," said Global. What Global means by protocol is that Freezo was not following the instructions.

"Now, I need a volunteer," Freezo said. "Who is brave enough to test the pH of this onion skin?" Behind his hulking shoulder, a beaker full of liquid began to bubble. The glass tube started to rattle, and a green vapor floated toward the ceiling. Vapor looks like smoke, but it's really liquid turning into a gas, like when you boil water for spaghetti.

"Sir," Global shot his arm up. "I don't think..."

"Ah! A victim! I mean a volunteer," the sub laughed at his joke. "Come on up!"

Global walked slowly toward that wackadoodle, looking back towards the class to save him. "No, what I mean, sir, is . . ." Global pointed to the beaker that was beginning to shake and bubble violently. Freezo turned around just in time to see the glass beaker literally (and what I mean by literally is that it actually happened) lift off the table.

The beaker looked like it had some kind of live animal jerking around inside, and then, it EXPLODED! Thick, snot-green liquid shot all over Colonel Freezo Freezingburg. Global turned around, and his goggles were covered in the stuff.

All of a sudden, the class, which had been nearly silent since Freezo walked in, erupted. Everyone roared with laughter at the outrageous experiment gone crazy-wrong.

My sister, Josephine, and her second-grade friends are all about making slime. It's a little too elementary for me, and by elementary, I mean babyish. But, just in case you don't already have the recipe, you can get everything you need at the dollar store. For five bucks, you can keep your siblings busy for at least an hour.

Okay, I'll admit it. I actually still love making slime. Just don't tell Josephine!

Super Slime Recipe

Here's what you need:

2/3 of a cup of white glue

1/4 cup of water

1 teaspoon of baking soda

2 cups of shaving cream

A few teaspoons of food coloring

1 1/2 tablespoons of contact lens solution
(make sure it contains boric acid!)

Here's what you do:

Mix the glue, water, baking soda, and shaving cream together. Then, add the food coloring and contact solution, and keep mixing!

CHAPTER 3

Frozen Students and One Clever Dummy

As the whole class was losing it over Freako Freezo, he began turning redder and redder. Global giggled as he removed his goggles and wiped them on his too small brown pants. Suddenly, Sir Freezo did something that was unexpected even for him. He grabbed his metal arm, twisted it off, and spiked it against the whiteboard! Something I'd seen on *Cops* zapped out where a hand should have been.

"Global!" I called, but it was too late. Freezo zapped him in the back with what I can only explain as a TASER-arm. Global froze in place, then teetered back and forth, and crashed to the floor.

Then, Sir Freezo ran toward me like the Terminator and ZAP! He shot me with the TASER-arm. I froze for a second from shock, but then, I realized I could still move. I jumped down under my table and began to crawl toward the back of the room as Freezo zapped and froze every kid in the class!

I peered at Freezo from under a desk. That maniac was sweating like a sheepdog on a hot summer day. Half-human, half-. . . what was he? Some kind of cyborg?

Then, a second question popped into my head. "Why didn't I freeze?" I wondered, as I looked around for a way to escape from this madman. My head was pounding, and I knew I was about to sneeze when I realized, "I have a fever!" A normal body temperature is 98.6 degrees Fahrenheit. Freezo couldn't freeze me because my body temperature was too high.

I was still trying to figure out how to get out of this classroom when the kid whose table I was under kicked me. "What the?"

A'lo's buggy eyes peered under the table. "Crawl to the window, Merlin. We outta' here!" he whispered. For once, A'lo's sleeping in class paid off. Freezo must have thought he was already frozen.

Slick as the cat he was, A'lo hurled a pencil against the door near the front of the classroom. Freezo was studying the broken beaker and mumbling, "Too much Carbon?" when he heard the pencil hit the door. He whipped his cinder block head away from us and toward the noise.

As soon as Freezo crept over to peek into the hallway, A'lo hissed, "Now, egghead!" I crawled as fast as I could on all fours to the window, turned the lever, and pushed it open. A'lo shoved me up and out like a gumball shooting out of the machine at Wal-Mart. For a pint-sized dude, he is surprisingly strong.

He wormed his way out behind me just as Freezo saw what was happening. Freezo charged toward us as I pulled on A'lo's arms. His pant loops had caught on the lever.

"Pull, you wimpy noodle!" A'lo yelled. I pulled, but not fast enough. Freezo reached out with his TASER-arm and zapped A'lo right on the butt!

"AHHHHH!" A'lo screamed, but he didn't freeze. The cellphone in his back pocket blocked the TASER. It's about time Alo's mama's old, deactivated cell phone that he's carried around since kindergarten had some use. I gave one more giant tug and pulled that little bully out of the window and into a dirt patch on the side of Washington Carver Elementary.

The window jammed shut, and Freezo banged on it like an angry orangutan. I reached out my hand to help lift A'lo from the ground. "Hey man, thanks for saving my skin."

A'lo slapped my hand back and said, "I wasn't trying to save you, Bruh! I just didn't want to die next to a loser named Merlin."

My ears started burning, and it wasn't my fever. "Well, you wouldn't have to if you'd just called me Big Monty!" I fumed.

Since we're on temperature—freezing students and my burning up forehead—check out this cool experiment. All you need are three glass jars, water, and food coloring. Fill one jar with hot water, one with cold, and one with water at room temperature. Now, drop a few drops of food coloring in each, and watch what happens.

Water molecules move differently based on their temperature. Any guesses which water will mix in the food coloring the fastest?

Let me give you a hint: cold water makes water molecules move very slowly. Now, what do you think?

Oh, you thought I was going to tell you? Heck no. Get out there and find out for yourself!

CHAPTER 4

Cyborg Students and a Search For Big Ace

A'lo jumped up quick as a cat with its tail on fire. We ran! Once we got out of Freezo's sight, I yelled, "We need to go get Principal Williams!"

A'lo wasn't having it. He likes to avoid Principal Williams as much as possible. "We don't need that tuxedo-wearing, mom-calling snitch to help us. I know how to take care of this psycho substitute."

Maybe A'lo was right. I remembered how unhelpful Principal Williams had been when the lunch lady went crazy. He was too busy practicing his wrestling poses to investigate when Mrs. Findlehorner made a monster to attack all the students who complained about her food! A'lo took off across the sidewalk toward the playground.

"Where are you going?" I looked back toward the school and my frozen classmates. We had to do something. Surprisingly, Alo's brain seemed to be working better than mine today, so I took off after him, which is something I thought I would never do.

The back of our playground connected to the parking lot of the high school. A'lo ducked down between the cars like he was some kind of superspy, and I followed him.

"Get down with your big lanky self!" A'lo hissed at me. "We've got to get my brother Big Ace in on this. Dude can build anything."

A'lo's brother was one of the scariest guys at Lincoln High School. Legend had it that Big Ace, AKA Antwann Jenkins, once stole a school bus with a bunch of kids on it while the driver flirted with Marina Tyler's mama.

"What do you think he can build to help with Colonel Cold?" I asked.

"A TASER-laser, you dope! What do you think?"

"Of course," I said. "A'lo, are you serious? A TASER-laser? We'd be lucky if we didn't kill ourselves with something like that."

"Go on back to Kindergarten, you ole' ghost runner," A'lo said. "I got this."

I couldn't risk Global's life on A'lo's TASER-laser idea, so I followed him. There was something else I didn't get. "A'lo, why do you care, anyway?" I asked him.

"Care?" his forehead wrinkled like a baby bulldog.

"Care about saving our classmates?" I asked. "You never help anybody except your group of boys. Not even them if you've got something better to do."

A'lo started laughing, "Bruh, you think I care about saving our classmates?" He held his stomach, fell on the ground, and started rolling around, laughing. "Jamal Tanner owes me ten bucks on last night's game, and if you think I'm not getting my cash at lunch today, you are c-c-c-crazy!"

Once A'lo caught his breath, we crept up to the back of the industrial arts building and looked into the window. Sparks of fire were flying everywhere. Kids in masks were building the body of a monster truck.

"I see him," A'lo said. "Only problem is we have to sneak past Tinker Troy."

"Tinker Troy?" I asked.

"The welding teacher, you book-fleeker." A'lo shook his head.

"Book-fleeker? Is that even a thing?" A'lo's insults were legendary.

"You ain't never heard of Tinker Troy? Big Ace says he turns kids into cyborgs. If he doesn't like a kid, the next thing you hear, that kid drops out of school. Everybody knows Tinker Troy is using them as dropout-cyborg-mechanics to build trucks that win every time at the motorsports racetrack." A'lo told this story like he was dead serious.

I couldn't help it. I laughed in his face!

"Oh, ok. Laugh. You're such a genius, but you can't figure out how to unfreeze your flabby friend or get my ten dollars back! You won't be laughing when a cyborg crushes that oversized brain of yours."

"Come on, A'lo," I distracted him. As a Sci-Fi lover I could have *owned* A'lo with my knowledge of cyborgs, but you don't want A'lo thinking up ways to get even with you for laughing at him. Dude is vicious and has a long memory. "Let's sneak in through Tinker Troy's office."

It seemed like I was surrounded by cyborgs today. First Colonel Freezo, and then, Tinker Troy's army of dropouts? I told you my school was weird.

SUPER
CYBERNETIC
GRAPPLER
ARM

ULTRA
LASER
TELESCOPIC
EYE

TITANIUM
LACED TRACTOR
LEG

Did you know, "cyborg" is really an abbreviation for cybernetic organism? If you don't know what "abbreviation" means, go back and read book one, Big Monty and the Lunatic Lunch Lady. Now, that was an adventure!

A cybernetic organism is a being with both organic and biomechatronic body parts. Organic means living, like the human Sir Freezo appeared to be. "Biomechatronic" means bringing together humans with machines. Biomechatronic scientists attempt to make devices that interact with human muscle, skeleton, and nervous systems. Somehow, the goofy Sir Freezo had figured out how to make himself into a cyborg!

Man, I love science. I told you I could run circles around A'lo! Now, you can too, not that it's so hard. That little dude is totally out of shape mentally and physically.

CHAPTER 5

Two Bad Brothers and One Flamethrower

We crept into the outside door of Tinker Troy's office that led to the industrial arts classroom. "How are we going to get Big Ace's attention with all that noise?" I asked.

You could hardly hear yourself think with the sounds of saws and welders whirring.

The only way you could tell this was an office was from the desk sitting in the middle of the room. Otherwise, it was full of bolts, spare machine parts, and rusty tools. It looked like a graveyard for discarded robots. I even thought I saw an arm that looked like Freezo's next to the coat rack in the corner.

My nose started to run, and I felt like I was going to sneeze. Maybe I should have stayed home today. "Wait a minute, did that thing move?" I asked A'lo, pointing to the coat rack.

"Shh," A'lo waved at his brother through a crack in the door, trying to get his attention. Big Ace held a blowtorch in his ripped arms and pointed it at an axle on the monster truck.

The coat rack jerked. "What in the world?" I stared in horror as jackets and sweaters began to slip off and onto the floor. "A'lo! It's moving!"

"Shut up, man," A'lo ignored me as he jumped up and down waving his arms at Big Ace, who didn't notice him through his welding mask. Just then, the coat rack crashed to the floor.

"Cyborg!" I screamed like a parrot in a room full of cats. A'lo whipped his head around, but it wasn't a cyborg. There was nothing human about it. This creature was some kind of low-budget robot. The coat-rack-robot crawled toward A'lo on blow torch hands, peering at him with flashlight eyes attached to its deflated basketball head. Its torso was made of an old-school boombox, and a wall clock hung around his neck by a rusty bicycle chain.

"It's nightmare Flava Flav!" A'lo yelled, backing up toward the desk.

The creature pulled its mismatched body to a full height of almost six feet tall. You will never believe what happened next. It turned a knob on its chest, and "In Da Club" started thumping out of it. The robot started jerking and sliding in some kind of rhythm. Was it moon-walking? That creature was dancing toward A'lo!

"Oh, you want some of this!" A'lo grabbed a broom and bowed up like a pee-wee ninja. Did he think he could fight this metal mound of a monster with a broomstick bo staff? A'lo swung his staff around like he'd been practicing for this moment his whole life! All of a sudden, A'lo did a straight-up standing backflip and landed on top of Tinker Troy's desk. He swung the broom over his head faster and faster and started yelling out, "Finish Him!"

I couldn't move as I watched A'lo crouch low like a dog doing his business in the park, ready to launch himself full-on street-fighter-style toward that Molly-Wopping mess.

Unfazed, the droid advanced toward A'lo and fired up its blowtorch hands. With one quick flame, it destroyed every straw on A'lo's broom. Just as I thought we were toast, Big Ace kicked the door open wearing a welding mask and carrying a flame canister in each hand. He growled, "Hasta la vista, Android!" Big Ace turned the flames up high and roasted that heavy metal, hip-hopping monster.

"Get outta here Lil' Dudes," Big Ace yelled. "Tinker Troy is coming, and ain't no flame thrower big enough to stop him." Big Ace turned around like nothing had happened and went back to class. A'lo and I ran for the door.

Man! And I thought elementary school was strange. Big Ace showed off his skills, but we still had classmates to defrost, and I didn't want anything more to do with Lincoln High School.

As we ran back to Washington Carver Elementary, it hit me. We needed brains more than muscles to face off with Sir Freeze-A-Lot. "A'lo, follow me."

CHAPTER 6

A Soccer Star and
a Dry Idea

We ran back toward Washington Carver. A'lo stopped and grabbed his side, "Cramp," he puffed. With his elbows on his knees and his face towards the ground, he struggled out, "What are we doing?"

I pointed toward the soccer field. A'lo glanced up, sweat dripping through the parts shaved into his eyebrows, to see a tiny girl covered in polka dots from socks to hairbows rocket a goal to the upper right 90 from beyond the midline.

"Bruh, seriously! We need help from your baby sister?"

"You mean the same baby sister that single-handedly fixed the school bus engine that broke down on the way to the Memphis Zoo? Or the baby sister that started the Mandarin Chinese Language Club in first grade? Or do you mean the baby sister that captured drone videos of the Midtown bank heist? If anyone can help us figure out Freezo, it's Josephine."

Before A'lo could argue with me, Josephine spotted us, shrieked, and ran over to hug me like she had not just seen me at breakfast this morning. "Josephine pleee-aaase stop hugging me at school."

Josephine stepped back, wiped her forehead with her polka dot wristband, and adjusted her eyeglasses. "Hey, Merlin! Did you boys come to cheer for me? What are you doing out of class?"

A'lo sneered, "Yeah, we snuck out of class to cheer for 2nd grade soccer. Are you kidding me?"

Josephine put her hand on her hip, just like our mom, looked A'lo straight in the eyes, and said, "Like you have anything better to do?"

"Listen, Josephine," I interrupted. "You'll never believe this unless you see it. We've got a popsicle-making cyborg for a substitute in Mrs. Curie's class. All the students are frozen like ice cubes. You have to help me unfreeze Global."

"Cyborg? Whatevs, Merlin. What side of YouTube have you been on lately?"

"I'm serious. He may not be a literal cyborg, but he has something attached where his arm should be that turns kids into ice cubes."

In disbelief, Josephine rolled her eyes, "Oh really? Then why are you two not part of the frozen food section?"

A'lo stepped forward and stuck his chest out like a puffed-up rooster. "I blocked Freezo's TASER with my brand new iPhone X like Kawhi Leonard blocked Lebron at the

AT&T center." A'lo bragged. "And Merlin . . . wait . . . why aren't you frozen, Big Brains?"

I felt my forehead with the back of my hand. I was burning hot, but I almost forgot I felt bad. "All I can think of is that my body temperature was too high to freeze."

"If you aren't joking, which I doubt very much, you'll need to freeze the freezer." Josephine's eyes narrowed like they did when she got an idea. "Boys, what's colder than ice?"

"The last pair of Jays I got," A'lo said as he wiped the top of his busted-up shoes.

"Think, Merlin. What's colder than ice?" Josephine gestured as if I could read her mind and waited for me to answer. I thought back to every NOVA episode I'd ever watched, but nothing came to mind. "Dry ice (CO_2), duh!" she said.

"Dry ice?" A'lo howled, holding his sides. "Dry like Merlin's ashy knees!"

I definitely should have stayed at home in bed with a box of Kleenex and that smelly stuff my mom rubbed on my chest. Anything was better than a whole day of listening to A'lo front on me.

———————————

How to Make Hot Ice

Try this one with a cool adult at your house. Here's how to make dry ice, or hot ice, at home. I adapted this one from the experiment I found online at: https://frugalfun4boys.com/hot-ice-science-experiment/

1. Combine 4 cups of vinegar and 4 tablespoons of baking soda in a pot. Add the baking soda a little at a time so that when it fizzes it won't overflow over the edges of your pot!

2. You have now made sodium acetate! (As well as carbon dioxide—it was given off in the reaction, which created all that fizzing.) You'll need to boil the solution to

reduce the amount of water so that it is concentrated enough to form crystals.

3. Cook your solution over low to medium heat for about an hour. You want to reduce it down to 1 cup or less. Some crystals should form in the pot.

4. Let the solution cool a little so it doesn't break the glass. Pour your sodium acetate into a glass container and put it in the refrigerator for 30 to 45 minutes.

5. Scrape off some crystals from the pot and put them on a tray or cookie sheet.

6. Pour the cooled solution SLOWLY onto the crystals that you scraped from the pan.

7. The ice is actually hot!

CHAPTER 7

A Fight with Freezo and a Second Science Flop

With Josephine's idea, I remembered a YouTube video I'd seen on how to make fog out of dry ice. Actually, it looks like fog, but it is really the gas coming off of solid carbon dioxide. Solid carbon dioxide is colder than frozen water. Companies use it to ship things like food because it goes directly from a solid to a gas when it melts. Regular ice turns into water when it melts, but dry ice just evaporates without any mess.

Dry ice was just the thing we needed to chill Freezo's TASER-arm, and thanks to YouTube, I knew just how to make it.

"Finally, you used that big brain for something," A'lo said. "I know how to get into the science supply closet. Follow me."

I followed A'lo down the hall as he dove and rolled behind corners like some kind of short Super Spy. "We need a pillowcase, duct tape, and a fire extinguisher," I called after him. I'd never seen A'lo have so much fun in school.

He wrinkled his forehead and put his finger to his lips, "shhhhh!" We rounded the corner and I watched as A'lo picked the lock of the supply closet with a mechanical pencil. Beakers, boxes, tubes, and all kinds of science equipment covered dust-lined shelves to the ceiling.

"Find a fire extinguisher and duct tape," A'lo ordered, like this was all his idea. "I'm going down to kindergarten to get a pillowcase off of one of those snot-nosed nappers."

I found a small fire extinguisher on the bottom shelf and duct tape in a box full of magnets. A'lo returned with a pink pillowcase covered in little white clouds.

"Dude, you're so wrong for taking that," I told him.

"You want to save your buddy and a whole class or worry about some little girl's rest hour?" A'lo said.

"You're straight," I thought of Global laid out on the classroom floor. "Let's go."

A'lo and I crept outside the door of our classroom and crouched below the window. We could hear Colonel Freeze smashing bottles and mumbling, "If only I could remember how to get this experiment right, I could be their inspiration!"

"Only thing that dude's gonna inspire me to do is learn Kung Fu," said A'lo as I handed him the fire extinguisher. I wrapped the opening of the soft pillowcase around the nozzle and duct-taped it tightly.

"On three, hold your breath, cover your eyes, and pull the trigger on the extinguisher," I told A'lo. I swear, for a second that tough little bugger looked scared, but just for a second. A'lo thumped his chest twice, took a deep breath, and squeezed the handle.

Whooosh! I held onto the pillowcase tight with some rubber cleaning gloves I swiped from the custodian's cart. The pillowcase expanded to twice its size.

Freezo heard the noise and threw open the classroom door. His TASER-arm hung two feet from my head, crackling and zapping.

"Now!" yelled A'lo, pulling the nozzle out of the pillowcase as I ripped off the tape and threw the contents right at the glowing TASER-arm. My stomach fell. Instead of a block of solid dry ice forming around Freezo's TASER, a powdery substance floated to the ground. Freezo's taser flickered and faded into a small light, but quickly crackled back to life.

"What went wrong?" A'lo shouted. He'd been knocked to the ground and was crab-walking backward out of Freezo's zapping range.

As soon as I saw the powder, I knew. The newer fire extinguishers used sodium bicarbonate instead of CO2. Someone had updated the extinguisher in the science closet.

"We're out of luck, Dude," I said as Freezo raised his TASER-arm and grinned. At least, if Freezo ended us, I wouldn't have to hear any more insults from A'lo.

Listen, I know making dry ice out of a fire extinguisher sounds pretty dope and all, but you probably want to skip that one unless you get attacked by a cyborg yourself. Have you ever heard of freezer burn?

Dry ice freezes at -109.3 Fahrenheit. To show you how cold that is, a person's core body temperature usually stays around 98.6 degrees Fahrenheit. You can start to freeze or experience hypothermia when your core body temperature gets to around 95 Fahrenheit or lower. Now, compare that to the temperature of dry ice. It's so cold it actually feels like it burns your skin if you touch it.

Dry ice actually freezes your skin cells, but it is treated medically just like a serious burn. So, if you ever do touch dry ice, make sure you wear really thick gloves!

CHAPTER 8

A Big Joker, A Little Joker, and A Hidden Ace

"Ha!" screeched Freeze. "So I'm not the only scientist whose experiments don't get the desired reaction? I don't Zinc so!" He laughed bitterly at A'lo, which is what saved us. That little dude does not put up with folks laughing at him.

"Oh, you got jokes?" A'lo stood up as tall as his three-foot self could stretch and said, "I know how to take care of this giant Cyborg Substitute. Freezo, yo' mama is so ugly, she made an onion cry!" he shouted.

Freezo's TASER fizzled. He looked stunned for a minute and then said, "Oh yeah? Well, your mama's so stupid, when she was working in the M& M factory, she threw away all the w's!"

A'lo was just getting started. "Oh, it's on, Freezo! Yo' mama's so stupid, they had to shut the school down to get her out of first grade."

"That is not true!" screamed Freezo, who was getting so mad that frothy white stuff was spraying out his mouth as he talked. "But, you know what is true? Your mama's so stupid, she was locked in the cafeteria and starved!" Freezo look proud of himself, and I got nervous.

My eyes had been darting between the duelers like a ping pong ball. A'lo's eyes looked like they were about to pop out his face. He was good, but so was Freezo.

Then, A'lo narrowed his eyes like a cat and spat out, "Yo' mama's so stupid, she tried to use a ruler to measure how long she could hold her breath!"

Freeze looked like he'd been hit with a two-by-four in the chest. That one knocked the wind out of him. He sucked in air and said, "Well, your mama's breath is so bad, she had to lock up her toothbrush to keep it from running away!"

I thought A'lo was going to explode all over Freezo. A'lo was so hot that his flat-top started to melt. Steam streamed off the top of his fresh fade. Nobody, and I mean nobody, beat A'lo at "yo' mama" jokes. Had he met his match?

A'lo breathed heavily, like some kind of bull about to charge, tensed up all his muscles, and yelled, "Yo' mama's breath is so bad, she has to photoshop it out of pictures!"

Freezo froze. He seemed stumped.

But, A'lo was on a roll. He really hit his stride, "And, yo' mama's so stupid, she put two quarters in her ears and thought she was listening to Fifty Cent."

A'lo waited, but Freezo had nothing. "And, your mama is so . . ." A'lo stopped. I looked at Freezo and couldn't believe what I saw. The substitute had sunk onto the floor and curled up into a ball like a little baby. Even the light on his TASER faded. Freezo was crying!

"You're right!" Freezo blubbered. "I don't know why I even care what you say about my mom. She was terrible to me!"

A'lo and I looked at each other.

"All I ever wanted to be was someone who could encourage kids because I never got that at home! All my mom did was put me down. The kids at school laughed at me too, and I never had friends, but I thought teaching would be a way to inspire kids to like all kinds of people. Turns out, kids are just as mean."

"Whoa, whoa, whoa," I jumped in. "You mean all that dancing around and joking you did at the beginning of class was to get us to like you?"

"Yes. I heard the way to win kids over was to be funny and cool," Freezo sniffled.

"Mr. Freezingberg, when I first saw you, I thought you were cool, with that scar on your face and your huge size, but then you started trying too hard," I said.

Alo's face softened. "Man, all you got to do is be you. Take it from me, everybody loves A'lo." I couldn't believe A'lo actually said something that made sense.

"Really?" Freeze said. "You think kids would like me for just me?"

"Trust me, Bruh," said A'lo. "You and that silver arm are Superfly material."

"Come on," I put my hand out to Freeze. "Let's go figure out what went wrong with that science experiment and wake-up the class."

———

I know it seems like "yo' mama" jokes are fresh. Actually, they are ancient. The first "yo' mama" joke dates back to 3500 BCE. That's over 5,000 years old! According to *The Huffington Post*, researchers in Babylon found a tablet that featured a few fairly inappropriate jokes revolving around mothers.

Also, a really old English dude named Shakespeare made a "yo' mama" joke famous in one of the plays he wrote. These jokes didn't actually say, "yo' mama," but they meant the same thing.

CHAPTER 9

A Scientific Solution and One Less Cyborg

A'lo and I followed Colonel Freeze back into the classroom where all the students sat, still frozen at their desks, except for Global, who was laid out on the floor with green goo clinging to his goggles.

"Sir Freezo, can you explain how your TASER-arm works, so we can defrost the class?" I asked him.

Colonel Freezo looked sad, "I'm not exactly sure. I took an online course on cryotherapy and had my buddy over in biomechatronics rig up this prosthetic arm in case anyone bullied me again. I'd gotten into some scary situations with bullies." What Freezo meant by prosthetic is an artificial body part, like a metal hand.

"So, you're not a cyborg?" A'lo asked.

"No. Just a guy who lost an arm serving my country and found a creative solution."

Cryotherapy. I wracked my brain. "Cryo" means producing extreme cold, and cryotherapy was healing through freezing parts of the body. All I could figure was that Freezo's arm was more powerful than he intended. "So, we need to heat them up?" I asked.

"I think that would work," said Freezo.

"But, how?" Too bad Global was frozen. He's like a walking Wikipedia. I bet Global would know how to solve this cryo-problem in a heartbeat.

A'lo's bad breath hit me in the face from over my shoulder, "You know who we need, Bruh."

"Global," I said.

"Global's on the block, like a cold block. Like TKO, Dude. Who we need is your baby sister." said A'lo, which was the smartest thing he'd said all day.

Just then, a bell rang, and students started pouring out of classrooms into the hallway. "Come on!" I waved A'lo and Freezo through the crowd of students toward the cafeteria. "Second graders are at lunch this period."

Freezo towered over the kids zig-zagging through the hallways. A'lo walked behind us, holding onto his pants, trying to pretend he wasn't with us. "On God, you are going to ruin my rep, Merlin." He muttered.

We paused outside the swinging cafeteria doors. Fifth-graders weren't allowed in the cafeteria during second-grade lunch. "How are we going to get Josephine out of lunch period?" I asked.

"Just let a professional handle this," A'lo said. He ran his hand over his flat-top, straightened his shirt, and busted into Washington Carver Cafeteria like he owned the place.

"What's he doing?" I asked Freezo who was tall enough to peek in the window.

"He's talking to her teacher," Freezo said. A minute later, A'lo swung the doors open and flashed his fillings at us. Josephine stood right behind him.

"This crazy guy comes in, telling some kind of story about how I'm the only kid in school who can tutor him in Mandarin Chinese, and Ms. Jenkins believed it!" Josephine cocked her eyebrow over her glasses and reminded me of our Grandma P., who always knew when we were up to something.

"Well, actually, you do speak a little Mandarin, right?" I reminded her.

"Of course, I speak Mandarin," sparked Josephine. "But, who in their right mind would believe A'lo wanted to learn anything?"

"Ouch, that's colder than Freezo!" A'lo said, but I think he took Jospehine's insult as a compliment.

"So, the dry ice worked?" Josphine asked, looking warily at Freezo's hand. By warily, I mean she looked at it like it might come to life any second and bite her. "You all are cutting into my highly precious social time," she said. "What do you need?"

Freezo and I explained the TASER-arm and cryotherapy to Josephine, and how it froze our classmates.

"Cryotherapy," she said. I could imagine the connections being made all over Josephine's brain. "So, all you did was lower their body temperature, which put them into some kind of mild coma?"

"Yeah, that's *all* he did," said A'lo rolling his eyes.

"So, all we have to do is thaw them out by reversing the probe temperature, or heating them up," Josephine concluded. Speaking of temperature, my forehead felt normal for the first time all day.

Freezo smiled. "Why didn't I think of that?" He took a tiny screwdriver out of his pocket and made three small adjustments to his prosthetic. It crackled to life, and A'lo stepped back. "No way am I going to be the victim, I mean volunteer, on this experiment," A'lo said.

CHAPTER 10

A Savvy Substitute and One Cool Ringtone

Back in the classroom, Freezo and I nodded at each other and bent down to Global's side. I held my breath as Freezo zapped him in the upper arm. Global sat bolt upright and said, "the pH of an onion skin is around 1.5. It's very acidic."

"He's back!" I said.

Slowly, we unfroze all the students, who seemed to remember nothing, which was really good for Freezo. After all, everyone deserves a second chance.

We took our seats, and Colonel Freeze began again. He taught us a pretty cool lesson on pH levels, and I even saw A'lo testing the pH level of Jasmine Flower's hair extension. She looked mad enough to slap him into next week, but A'lo actually looked excited about school for once.

"And that," said Colonel Freezo, "is how you test the pH of common household objects."

The class clapped, which was strange, but maybe somewhere in their subconscious minds they were thankful to be defrosted. Global turned to me in his science goggles and said, "Not too bad for a substitute teacher. I hope we have him again sometime."

I caught A'lo's eye at the back of the room, and even that hard little joker was smiling.

After class, I stayed behind to help Colonel Freeze clean up. "I guess I don't need to make jokes to make kids like me," he said.

"Or dance," I reminded him.

He nodded and gave me his Raiders cap. We walked to lunch together. I saw A'lo hitting up Jamal Tanner for his cash ahead of us.

"One more thing," I said, pointing to Colonel Freezo's pocket. "We have got to change that ringtone on your cell phone. There are some things kids won't forgive."

"Note taken by this substitute," Freezo said, "Thanks for everything, Merlin."

I should have told Freezo that without Josephine and A'lo, of all people, the class would still be frozen. As we walked into the cafeteria for fifth-grade lunch, all I said was, "Call me Big Monty."

Hey Reader,

Matt Maxx here. I'd love to hear from you! Ask me your science questions, or tell me what you thought of the book. I'd love to hear your idea for the next villain Big Monty needs to deal with. Just send me an email at whoismattmaxx@gmail.com, or have your parents jump over to our Facebook and Instagram pages, Matt Maxx Books, and send me a picture of yourself with this book!

Peace Out, Matt Maxx